Unde~ ~~
Bomber

and Other ~~

Written by
David Clayton, Barry On and Eric Johns

Illustrated by Elsie Lennox

Contents

Under the Bomber's Moon

by David Clayton

1 Bad news from London

On and on, the bombers were coming,
flying high above the silver sea. On and
on, the planes were coming, engines
humming, heading for England.

In Manchester, David huddled by the
crackling fire. The only other sound was the
quiet ticking of the clock on the mantelpiece.

Apart from the fire, there was no other light in the living room above the grocery store. David, his gran and Mum leaned towards the radio as Gran fiddled with the dial. David broke the silence.

'Please let me go and look for Prince,' he said.

An hour before, David had gone down to the coal shed to fetch some coal for his gran. Prince had been jumping about all over the place. When David turned, the yard gate was open and the dog was gone. It was strange, not like Prince at all. He was a lazybones, hanging around to beg for scraps. There was no food out there in the cold, empty streets. Where would he go to and why?

Just then, the crackly radio announcer's voice broke into David's thoughts. He sounded very serious.

'This is the BBC Home Service and here is the news...'

They all leaned even further forward.

'Bombing has been heavy in the London area...,' the man began.

'Isn't Dad in London?' David looked at his mum.

His gran gave him an angry glance.

'Near London. Shush!'

'But he hasn't written for three weeks!' said David. 'Perhaps something has...?'

'Don't worry,' said his mum, 'it'll just be the post. There is a war on! Letters take ages these days.' Then she looked away into the fire to hide her eyes.

'Cities in the Midlands have also been hit...,' the bad news went on and on.

'Maybe it'll be our turn tonight,' said Gran.

'Time for bed.' David's mum didn't want him to hear any more bad news, any more about bombing and burning.

'But what about Prince?' David asked. 'We can't leave him out there!'

'We can have a quick look up and down the street if you like,' said his mum when the news was over. 'He can't be that far away.'

But when they stood in the street under the bright moon, there was no hairy mongrel in sight.

'Prince! Prince!' he had called – but nothing.

While they were standing there, the air-raid warden, a tough old man in a tin hat, came stomping up.

'Have you seen Prince, Mr Holt?' David asked.

'Well,' said the man, 'there was a dog that looked like Prince down... let me see ... down near Potter's Pet Shop.' Then he turned and looked at the sky. 'Look at that, a "bomber's moon", lighting us up, bright as day. But we've been lucky so far...'

But at once, a siren started howling to the east towards the Derbyshire Hills.

'Spoke too soon,' he grumbled. 'You'd better get inside! And don't forget to draw your curtains.'

Poor Prince! thought David. Outside at the mercy of the bombers. Gran had been right. It *was* Manchester's turn to suffer.

2 Bedtime escape

'Did you say near the pet shop?' David called as Mr Holt limped away. The boy had taken one step in that direction when his mum grabbed him by the arm.

'No!' she said. 'In!'

'Prince will get killed!' he cried.

'He'll be all right,' said his mum. 'It might be a false alarm anyway.'

'But MUM...,' David tried again, but it was no use.

'Come on, it's far too dangerous to be outside now.'

She led him up through the living room and up the dark, twisty staircase to the attic, way above the grocery shop. When the war first started, they used to sleep in the cellar but it was cold and smelly. They would go down there, get cold and there would be no raid. Now, they were tired of carting things up and down stairs. They just went to bed as usual and took a chance.

Outside, the nearest sirens started up. The city was just silver roofs under the light of the moon. David opened the window to see if he could spot Prince but there was a shout from below.

'Get that light out! They'll be here in
no time!'

Mr Holt wasn't pleased with him.
Lights sometimes gave bombers something
to aim at. Tonight they didn't need lights.
The whole city was bathed in moonlight.

David's mum closed the window.

'Don't worry! We're miles from the
docks and the railway yards. They might
leave us alone,' she said biting her lip.

David took one last peep through the
curtains. For a moment, he thought he saw
a dog moving in the shadows.

'Look, there's Prince!' David shouted, but
when his mum looked, the street was empty.

'He'll be all right!' she said, pulling the curtains to, again. 'Dogs have nine lives!'

'That's cats, Mum!' he said. '*Cats*!'

'Oh, yes,' she said giving him a little kiss, 'so it is. Good night!'

''Night, Mum!' he said.

She slipped away, giving him a careful look as she went out.

But the second she was gone, David made his plans. There was no way that he would sit at home while Prince was in such danger. However, he couldn't just go charging downstairs and out. His mum was crafty. He knew *just* what she'd do. He stayed put under the covers. Every second seemed like an hour. Come on, Mum! Come on! he thought.

Ten minutes later, he heard the door click as she came up to check on him. Time to snore like a saw mill.

ZZZZZZZZZZZZZZZZZZZZ!!!!!!!!!!

The door clicked again. Her feet bumped down the steep stairs. Then the door at the bottom of the stairs banged. Finally, Mum's bedroom door clumped shut. YES!

Time to find Prince. The room felt cold, very cold. Somehow he couldn't get out of it fast enough. It was strange, almost as strange as the way Prince had run off. Normally the attic was warm from the fire below, but not today. Something bad is going to happen tonight, David thought. I can feel it!

Quickly, he slipped into his clothes, crept inch by inch down the stairs, across the living room, past the dying fire, down the back stairs and out into the yard. The gate shut with a loud CLACK! No time to turn back now even if Mum heard. He was *really* going to get it if she caught him out here.

Two steps past the gate, he felt the hairs on his neck stand up. Far away, he could hear the engines of the bombers as they came humming through the night.

3 Night on fire

David glanced both ways down Swallow Street. No sign of Prince, but there was something moving. A cigarette burned like a glow-worm in a factory doorway to the left. Mr Holt was smoking, waiting for the bombing to start.

I wish he'd go away, David thought. If I

call Prince now, he'll hear me. What am I going to do? Slowly, slowly he sneaked to the right towards Charles Street and Potter's Pet Shop.

But a moment later, he didn't have to worry about making too much noise any more.

SWISH! A great beam of white searchlight spiked up into the sky; then another and another, sweeping the sky, hunting for silver dots, deadly silver dots, planes full of bombs.

CRACK-CRACK-CRACK-CRACK! Now the anti-aircraft guns in the brewery yard started to smack their bullets into the sky. Something glittering and tiny was caught in the light high above. A PLANE! Imagine! That shiny thing was a bomber! David had never seen an enemy plane before. There were Germans in it! Real Germans! Here, over Swallow Street.

CRUMP! CRUMP! CRUMP! Loud noises filled the air. Bombs were falling but not very close. It wasn't like London on the radio. This was here. This was now! Real and not scary at all, just exciting, so exciting.

Then David thought about Prince again, about Potter's Pet Shop.

SHEEEEEEE!!!!!!! KERRRUMPP!!!!!!
The ground shook. Closer!
KERRRUMPP!
Very close!

David heard a shout behind him but he was off without looking back.

Charles Street was straight across from Swallow Street. Nosher, his friend, lived there, as well as Mr Potter. David ran like mad, past the Ram's Head pub and on into his friend's twisty street.

WHAM! Suddenly, he was flat on the ground with the cobbles digging into his back. Red and orange fire leapt up like a great tree into the sky above him. Smoke swirled like something out of a pantomime.

The bomb had hit the garage way down beyond the pet shop. The blast wave had rattled David's bones and flattened him. He got up, stiff and aching, and limped on. The back of his head hurt. It didn't seem like a game any more.

'PRINCE! PRINCE!' he croaked, but smoke hid the street except for a glow at the far end.

SHEEEE!!!!!! WHAP! Another bomb had fallen ahead of him. There was no explosion but David felt the shockwave run under his feet. Hot air frizzled his face and dried his eyeballs until they were tight. It wasn't fun any more! No fun at all, this war.

Ahead the sky was red above the station. Fire engines came jangling up from Mersey Square. Bits of shell rattled on the roofs. The smell of burning filled David's nose. CRACK! CRACK! The guns chipped away again. It all spun around in his aching head like horrible jangly music from a fairground roundabout.

One more corner and … what luck … only the garage and the firelighter factory on the left side of Charles Street blazed. The houses had just lost windows. But then David went cold, in spite of the sizzling heat.

On the right, just before the end of the street, Mr Potter's shop lay smashed like an eggshell. But it was not on fire. Something had hit it. All one end had fallen down.

On and on he ran. By now, some people were pouring out of their houses to see what was on fire. Others ran away with blankets wrapped round them. One lady carried a budgie in a cage. There was a lot of confusion and people were shouting. But David had eyes only for the pet shop.

One end of it seemed to have fallen into the cellar.

David heard birds squawking, cats mewing and a dog, one dog barking. But it was down there, under the ruin.

'Prince!' he yelled. 'PRINCE!!!'

But only the birds replied. Now the barking had stopped.

'PRINCE!' he yelled again.

Then he noticed a hand sticking out from under the rubble. It was moving. Then a dusty head appeared.

'Mr Potter?' he shouted.

BOOOOOOOOOOOOOM!!!!!!!

As the boy reached down, the firelighter factory blew up behind him. He felt his hair scorch and his neck burn. Then everything went black.

4 The bomb

When David opened his eyes, everything was still black. He was lying face down. His head hurt and his face was wet. Blood? No. Something was licking his face.

'Prince?' he said, but he couldn't see a thing.

He was stuck. He wriggled and …

CRASH! He was on a hard floor. His head was booming now.

'Prince?' he repeated. But no. It was Max, Mr Potter's white Labrador. Prince must still be out there! Then he saw shiny black metal in the orange light from above and his heart nearly stopped. A bomb, an *unexploded* bomb!

'David …' a faint voice came from the shadows. Mr Potter lay with his arm trapped by something. 'Pull … that … lever … gas.'

David had been more bothered about the shop falling down on him. Now he had a bomb *and* gas escaping in a street full of flames. He slipped across and dragged at the lever. Click! It was closed.

'Door …'

Now Mr Potter was pointing to a small worn cellar door quite close to the fin of the bomb. So, maybe the bomb disposal men could get in that way.

David was worried. 'I'll see to you first.'

But Mr Potter waved his hand and shook his head. 'Door …' he croaked again.

So, over David went, slowly, carefully, gently. And so did Max!

'No, Max, no!!! STAY!!!!'
Why was Max such a pest? The dog
flopped down on the floor and sighed
loudly.

It was very quiet down there now: quiet and stinky and scary. The birds had calmed down a bit. Outside, bells were ringing, voices shouting and a siren marked the end of the raid. It was all far away like echoes in a dream, but the shiny cylinder of the bomb next to him was no dream.

Unbolt the door, push the door – nothing.

David squeezed himself between the bomb and the door so that he could push harder. He felt the cold metal of the bomb fin against his neck. Icy fingers seemed to run all over him, he could hardly breathe.

One more try...

CRUNCH!

The cellar door burst open.

Two metres above, he saw a square of fiery sky. Max suddenly appeared next to him and leapt up to street level.

'Hey!' yelled somebody. 'That's the old man's dog!'

Heavy boots came clumping down the side. Many hands dragged David clear.

'Well, done, lad! Anyone else down there?'

'Mr Potter's stuck and there's a bomb right near the door!'

Carefully, so carefully, the rescuers slipped down the hole and past the bomb. Then they dug gently until Mr Potter's arm slipped free from some fallen shelves.

'Thank you! Thank you so much!' he said.

'We're not out of it yet,' said the nearest rescuer. 'The bomb's still live!'

A long minute later, Mr Potter staggered out on to the street.

'David, David!' he said, hugging the boy.

It was time for David to carry on his search, but now every bone in his body seemed to ache. Where was Prince? Then another dreadful feeling ran right through him and he hopped and limped back round the corner until he got to Swallow Street.

He looked across in the glow to his house. He looked, and looked again. He knew that his attic window was the highest point around. He *had* to be able to see it – but he couldn't. The shop was gone!

Suddenly, David was running, dragging his tired body on and on. He bumped into people who crowded the streets. He tripped over hose pipes that lay like snakes across the road. He was running wildly, running blindly.

Finally, he came to where his house should have been. The top two floors were missing. The rest was a ruin, even worse than the pet shop. Nobody could live through that.

'Mum! MUM!!!!!' he yelled, but the crowd just looked at him.

'AAAAAAA!!!!!!!' he cried as raced away into the blazing town.

5 Surprises

David zig-zagged through the smoky streets. He ran and ran and ran. Finally, he crashed into a huge man in a big hairy coat.

'All right, son?'

'My…! My…all gone! GONE!' he howled.

'Okay, son. Take it easy!' The man's voice was kind, warm.

He felt himself being picked up like a baby – carried over the huge man's shoulder. Next thing he was sitting in front of a warm fire.

FIRE! The night had been all fire. He felt the man place a blanket around his shoulders. Even so, David couldn't stop shaking. He was handed a mug of soup but he didn't feel hungry. He just felt empty and alone. Slowly, he looked around. He saw a high ceiling, tall windows and desks and chairs. He realised he was sitting in his own school, in his own classroom – Miss Murphy's room!

'You all right, son?' a smiling woman in a grey uniform was sitting by him.

He looked around. There were dozens of camp beds.

Then the events of the night leapt up
in his mind – Prince, the fires, the bombs,
the shop…

'It's been a bad night,' the woman said.

David was going to say something but
the words stuck in his throat. He was never
short of something to say but now his

mouth wouldn't work. There was nothing to say. It was the end of his world.

There was a noise outside the door. Two men were arguing and a dog was barking. Then women's voices joined in.

'You can't come in here with a dog,' a stranger was saying.

'We *must* look in there. He's been missing all night,' an old woman's voice replied.

Suddenly, David saw a brown hairy shape hurtling towards him and the next thing he knew, something was licking his face.

'PRINCE!'

He wasn't alone. Prince had made it.

'David! DAVID!' Someone was shouting from the door. He turned and ran. It was Mum – and Gran!

'Mum! Oh, Mum!'

The room was spinning. David's head felt like it was bursting, his heart exploding.

Mum grabbed him and nearly crushed him with her hug.

Then Gran joined in and squashed him completely even though she had her arm in a bandage.

'Oh, David, where have you been?' said Mum. 'We've been looking for you half the night! Why didn't you stop when I shouted? We heard the gate bang and followed you. Gran was hurt when the garage got hit. We saw Mr Potter at the hospital and he told us he saw you in his cellar.'

Suddenly, David felt all wobbly and weak.

'Oh, Mum!' was all he could say.

Then Prince was licking his leg and he heard a deep voice behind him.

'DAVID!'

It couldn't be, it just *couldn't*, could it? He was in London, wasn't he?

But, no! There was his dad, tall, slim and fair, snatching him up and twirling him round.

'Oh, David. Thank goodness you're safe. I got up to Manchester with the Birmingham firemen. All that was left of the shop was a pile of rubble and I thought you were all gone…' He didn't finish as tears ran down his face.

'We all met up at the hospital,' said Gran.

'It was my last hope,' said Dad.

'OOOOOOh, Dad!!!!'

And when his dad put him down, David turned to Prince.

'Oh, Prince!' he said giving him a cuddle. Then he thought about the ruin where they would have been sleeping, but for the dog. 'You knew it was going to happen all the time, didn't you, Prince?' he said.

In what way is Prince a hero?

Albert

by Barry On

Chapter 1

Peter stopped pedalling for a moment to watch a lone Hurricane flying low over the fields of ripe wheat ahead of him. You could always tell a Hurricane from a Spitfire – the fuselage curved back from the cockpit to the tail instead of going in a straight line. Peter thought the Spitfire was the better aircraft; but the Hurricane was pretty good too. He had balsa wood models of both planes hanging in his bedroom. The plane disappeared noisily over the horizon and Peter continued cycling towards Harper's farm.

He went to Harper's farm every weekend at this time of the year to help with the harvest. There was a shortage of farm labour because of the war, and as John Harper was his uncle it was also a matter of helping the family. To be honest, he was not all that fond of his uncle. The farmer was a hard taskmaster and inclined to be short-tempered. Peter disliked the way that he sometimes swore at the two big cart horses, Winston and George, if they struggled to get the laden wagon up a steep rise in the field. Once he had even jabbed at Winston with a pitchfork and drawn a little blood. 'Leave him alone. He's doing his best,' Peter had wanted to say but didn't dare. However, he noticed that later that day his uncle had patted Winston on the neck and said words of praise in his ear. John Harper might be stern, but he was usually fair.

Billy Harper came out to see Peter as he put his bike in the open barn. Billy was John Harper's son and went to the same school as Peter. He eyed Peter with the smug face of someone who knew something the other didn't – something important.

'You'll never guess what we've got on the farm.'

Peter was determined not to be impressed, whatever the news. 'Horses? A tractor? Elephants? Martians?'

'Don't be stupid,' sneered Billy. 'Nothing like that.' He drew a deep breath. 'We've got a Nazi on the farm. A real Nazi.'

'What on earth are you talking about?' Peter imagined a black-uniformed, peak-capped officer with a swastika armband and a Hitler salute. 'We haven't been invaded, have we?'

''Course not, stupid. He's a prisoner of war.

He was a soldier – a German soldier. He fought against us. Now he's got to help us.'

Billy was almost crowing with pleasure. Peter looked at him with distaste. Perhaps he didn't like his uncle much, but he did respect him. He neither liked nor respected his cousin. Billy liked to think Peter was his friend – he wasn't.

They walked across the fields together towards the sound of the tractor already hard at work towing the reaping machine that cut and bound the yellow sheaves of wheat and dropped them on to the short stubble.

'That's him,' pointed out Billy, 'that's the Nazi.'

There was a solitary figure in the far corner of the field lifting pairs of sheaves and setting them upright in sets of three pairs, heads together, with a further sheaf at each end. Stooking, it was called. The ears of wheat were left to stand and dry out in the sun before they were carted off and built into stacks. It was hard work, but Peter enjoyed it.

Peter eyed the figure cautiously. The man was short and stocky. He wore dark trousers and a cloth jacket with a large blue

patch sown on to the back. His brown hair
was balding and he looked about the same
age as Peter's own dad who was an air
force mechanic.

'Doesn't look much
like a Nazi,' he said
to Billy. 'Just looks
ordinary to me.'

''Course he's a
Nazi,' scoffed Billy.
'They're all Nazis,
aren't they?'

Peter might have replied, but John
Harper waved at them impatiently from the
cab of the tractor and the two boys separated
and set to work. Through the morning the
sun rose higher and hotter and the tractor
never paused in its tireless journey round
and round the slowly diminishing acres of
standing wheat. Even three workers could
barely keep pace with its progress, but
Peter noticed that the German prisoner of
war, although never seeming to hurry, still
seemed to manage to work much more
quickly than either of the boys.

At about eleven o'clock, Peter saw the welcome sight of Mrs Harper walking briskly across the fields from the farmhouse carrying a basket containing a jug of cold tea and mugs. The engine of the tractor stopped at last and the two young workers stretched out gratefully under the shadows of a line of large elms that marked the edge of the field. John Harper walked back with his wife to the farmhouse to attend to some business. The German walked over to the shade and sat down silently a few feet away.

Peter studied him curiously. The only German soldiers he had seen before were in comics or in films. They wore steel helmets that covered the backs of their necks, unlike the round tin hats of the British Army. They were portrayed as cruel and humourless, used words like *schweinhund*, and despite their ruthless efficiency were always beaten in the end by the less organised but more inventive bravery of the British.

The man looked up and met Peter's stare. His eyes were brown and they seemed quietly amused at Peter's interest. He pointed to his chest.

'Albert,' he said.

Then he pointed a finger at Peter with a question in his eyes. Peter coloured slightly. His mother had always told him it was rude to stare.

'Peter,' he answered. 'My name is Peter.'

The man nodded. 'Ja.' He repeated the name, only he made it sound like 'Payter'.

Billy sniggered. Then he scowled. 'You're not supposed to talk to him. He's the enemy. You're not supposed to fraternize with the enemy.'

'Don't see what harm it can do,' said Peter. 'Anyway, we shan't be doing much talking, I can't speak German and I don't suppose he can talk English. But I'd like to talk to him if I could.'

Albert had been following this little exchange of words without showing any emotion. He looked at each boy in turn. Then he gave Peter another brief nod, as though in approval.

'Payter,' he murmured. He reached in the pocket of his jacket and took out an old curved pipe. He stuck it in his mouth and sucked the stem thoughtfully. The bowl of the pipe was empty. Then he felt in the other pocket and took out a flat piece of wood, about five inches square, and a very small pocket knife. Carefully and skilfully he began to work with his knife on the surface of the wood. Peter tried to imagine him in a steel helmet. It was difficult. Then the farmer returned and called them back to work.

Chapter 2

During the week that followed, Peter thought a lot about the lonely German working on his uncle's farm. He told his mother about Albert. She told him to be careful of Germans. His mother worked behind the counter at the local newsagents. He asked her whether she could get him some tobacco for Albert.

'Tobacco?' For a German soldier? Whatever next?'

But the following Saturday morning, as Peter was getting out his bike to cycle to the farm, she put a small paper bag in his hand.

'You'll get me the sack,' she said. Then she smiled a little sadly. 'I hope he enjoys it. I don't suppose he gets a lot of pleasures at the moment.'

Peter looked inside the bag, thanked his mum and rode off. By the time he reached the farm the sun had disappeared and the first few spots of rain were beginning to fall.

Soon a heavy summer shower swept over the fields and all outside work was suspended.

Albert was set the task of chopping logs in the big barn and Peter was told to clean some horse brasses there. John Harper and Billy stayed in the house.

Peter rubbed away at the brasses and watched Albert setting up the logs and splitting them expertly with single blows. Alone in a barn with a German soldier armed with a sharp axe! If Billy were right, then he was in mortal danger. At least John Harper seemed to have no fears about leaving him in the company of Albert. He grinned to himself.

When it was almost time for a break, he walked over to Albert and held out the paper bag that his mother had given him. The German seemed surprised.

'Für mich?'

'For you,' Peter nodded, 'from my mother.'

'Deine Mutter?'

'Yes. I mean, Ja.'

Albert turned the paper bag over in his hands in the way that grown-ups often do when they are given something unexpected, as if they are trying to guess what is in it without opening it. Then he carefully took out the contents. Inside was a packet of Erinmore tobacco and a box of Bryant and May matches. Albert's eyes lit up with surprise and pleasure. He reached out and shook Peter's hand solemnly.

'Danke. Thank you. Much. And thank you, Payter's Mutter.'

He took the pipe from his pocket and filled it lovingly with his stubby fingers. He

struck a match and soon the fragrant smoke of the tobacco floated in the air of the barn. Albert gave a deep sigh of pleasure.

There were footsteps outside the barn. It was Billy bringing the tea – hot this time. He sniffed the air.

'Smoking? In the barn? Don't you know better than that?'

'It's quite safe,' Peter told him. 'Albert knows what he's doing.'

'Is that so?' said Billy, sarcastically. 'Then I suppose it's all right if I have a smoke too.'

He reached in his side pocket and took out a crumpled packet of Woodbines and a half empty box of matches. He lit a cigarette with inexpert fingers and puffed out a cloud of acrid blue smoke. He coughed slightly.

'Want one?' He proffered the packet to Peter. Peter shook his head.

Albert watched silently. Then he took out his carving and began to work on it. Peter went over to watch. It was a design of trees with interweaving branches, sheaves of wheat, and horses. In the centre of the design was a large *B*. It was almost finished.

'It's beautiful,' breathed Peter. 'Who is it for?'

The German ran his hand over the carved wood.

'Für mein Sohn. Boris.'

He took from his inside pocket a creased photograph. It was of a boy just a little younger than Peter, with brown curly hair smiling into the camera.

'Boris,' he told Peter. He seemed very proud of his son.

'Very nice,' said Peter. He would have liked to have said more, to have questioned him more, but he didn't know the words.

Chapter 3

Two weeks later the harvesting was all done, the tall stacks had been built from the dry sheaves of wheat, and smaller stacks had been made with the hay that would be winter feed for the farm animals of the neighbourhood.

Albert had been hard at work scything the long grass at the edge of a meadow with long, skilful strokes, while Peter and Billy laboured with bill hooks to clear a ditch of summer weed.

At the mid-morning break they sat leaning against the hay that was already bone dry after days in the hot sun. Albert sucked his pipe and carved at his wood. Peter watched him. When it was time to resume their tasks, Billy stayed behind for a while and did not rejoin Peter for several minutes.

It was only a short while later when Peter happened to glance back that he saw something that made his heart leap in panic. A wisp of blue smoke was curling upwards from the pile of hay where they had been resting.

'Fire!' he shouted. 'The hay's on fire!'

Albert dropped the scythe and hurried
over to the hay. He grabbed a pitchfork and
began pulling out clumps of smouldering
hay and stamping on them. Billy ran for
his father. Peter raced to fetch water.

With John Harper's help the fire was
soon put out and no great harm had been
done. But fire was the peril that the farmer
feared most on his farm and he was very
angry.

'I could have lost the lot,' he shouted
angrily. 'All that winter feed gone up in
smoke. And in wartime, when every bit of
hay is precious.' He glared at the two boys.
'How did it happen? Fires like that don't
start from nothing.'

Peter spread his hands helplessly, but
Billy, pink-faced, pointed an accusing
finger at the German prisoner of war.

'It was him – Albert. It must have been. He was smoking his pipe by the hay.'

Albert was standing holding the pitchfork. His face was blackened with smoke. He looked at Billy but he showed no emotion.

'Is that true?' demanded John Harper. 'Do you have a pipe?'

'Pipe? Ja.'

The German took the pipe from his pocket and showed it to the farmer.

'You should know better than that.' John Harper seemed very disappointed as

well as angry. 'You're a farmer yourself. You know the danger.'

'I expect he did it on purpose,' accused Billy. 'Sabotage and all that.'

The farmer's eyes hardened at the thought. 'You're in real trouble now, Albert. When I tell the authorities about this you won't be getting any more outside work. You'll be in the lock-up.'

Billy sniggered maliciously. Peter stared at Albert in despair. Then he looked suddenly at Billy and realised the truth. He turned to the farmer.

'No!' Peter cried.

His uncle waved a dismissive hand. 'You can't save him now, Peter.'

'But it wasn't Albert. It couldn't have been.'

'Shut up,' hissed Billy warningly.

'Why couldn't it have been?' asked the farmer.

'Because he wasn't smoking his pipe,' replied Peter. 'It was empty. He was only sucking it. He must have been out of tobacco.'

'Well, if it wasn't Albert, who was it?'

Peter felt the German's eyes looking at him – patient, waiting. He swallowed hard.

'It must have been Billy,' he muttered unwillingly. 'He must have been having a smoke behind the hay when we went back to work.'

Billy was furious. 'You sneak!' he cried. 'I'm your friend. I'm English. You'd tell lies about me to save a Nazi? You're a traitor.'

The farmer fixed Billy with his stern eyes. 'Turn out your pockets.'

Billy reddened and blustered, but he knew better than to disobey. He reluctantly took from his pocket an almost empty packet of cigarettes and a box of matches. 'But it wasn't me,' he whined hopelessly.

'Get inside,' commanded his father. 'I'll deal with you later.' Then he turned to the

others. 'You two get back to work. We've wasted enough time already.' He strode back to the farmhouse in the wake of his unhappy son.

Albert laid aside his pitchfork. Then he walked over to Peter. He took Peter's hand in his own firm grip.

'Danke,' he said. 'Danke, Payter.'

Chapter 4

It was a few weeks before Peter cycled over to the farm again on an errand for his mother. The sky was overcast, the stubble fields had been ploughed into long furrows of dark earth and there was no sign of Albert.

'There's no more work for a farmhand here,' explained Mrs Harper. 'Albert's gone to work on a pig farm.'

She smiled at Peter. 'He left something for you. He said it was for his friend, Payter.'

She handed him a small packet about five inches square. 'He was a nice enough fellow,' she said, 'for a German.'

Peter didn't need to turn the packet

over in his hands. He knew at once what it contained. When he opened it, he saw that the carving had been finished – with one alteration.

The *B* had been turned into a *P* – *P* for Peter. Or Payter. He smiled. Whatever it stood for, it stood for him.

Do you think it was right for Peter to befriend Albert?

Alf the Spycatcher

by Eric Johns

1 Spying on the spy

The spy limped down the stairs clutching a bag to his chest. Alf and Vera stopped breathing as he passed their hiding place. The spy suspected nothing. He went on down the next flight of stairs and out the front door.

'You know what to do?' Alf whispered, as soon as he heard the door open.

Vera looked worried but nodded. Her curly hair bobbed up and down.

Alf ran up the attic stairs to the spy's flat. On the landing, at the top, was a cooker and a cupboard with a lock on it, where the spy kept his food and ration book.

The spy was Mr Kolenski. He had gone to put some rubbish in the dustbin at the back of the house. Alf pushed open the door to his flat. He knew he only had a few seconds to find some proof that would convince his mum that Mr Kolenski was a German spy.

Alf glanced round the room. The flat was in the roof and the ceiling sloped. There was only one small window and the room was dark and creepy. He wasn't sure what he was looking for. In the film he'd seen last week, there had been a spy and in his hide-out there'd been a message written in code. If he could find something like that everyone would have to believe him.

There was a small table with some paper on it. He crossed the room quickly. A floorboard creaked. That was the one he could hear in his bedroom. Every night he lay in bed and listened to the spy limping up and down above his head for what seemed like hours.

Alf tried to read what was written on the paper but it was in another language. He wondered if it was German. It didn't look like the message in the film; there'd been columns of carefully printed letters in that.

He looked round for something else. On a chair in a corner was a small suitcase. There was a loop of wire hanging out of it. In the film the spy had a suitcase exactly like that, and in it there'd been a wireless transmitter for sending radio messages to Germany.

Alf heard footsteps coming up the first flight of stairs. He hesitated, then took a step towards the suitcase. The floorboard creaked. He froze. The spy's footsteps reached the first floor landing.

Alf heard Vera say, 'Would you like to see my doll?'

He sighed with relief. She'd remembered her lines.

Alf took his foot off the creaky floorboard, then his nerve failed and he fled on tiptoe to the door. He would investigate the case another time, but he had no doubt that there was a wireless transmitter in the suitcase.

As he slid through the door he heard Mr Kolenski saying, 'Zat is a pritty doll, Vera.'

Alf squeezed into the space between the cooker and the cupboard.

The spy climbed heavily up the stairs and went into his flat without glancing at the dark corner of the landing. His door closed.

Alf let out his breath and padded downstairs to where he and Vera lived with their mum.

2 Alf stands alone

'He's got a little suitcase with a wireless in it,' Alf told his mother excitedly.

Vera nodded.

'Oh, yes,' their mum said, scraping a carrot.

'You're not listening,' Alf protested.

'Yes, I am, dear.'

'Well, why's he got a secret wireless if he isn't a spy?'

His mum sighed. 'Why's who got what?'

Alf forced himself to be patient. 'Mr Kolenski, upstairs. Why's he got a wireless if he isn't a spy?'

'To listen to the news, I expect.'

'But it's in a suitcase,' Alf repeated. 'It's a transmitter.'

'Like in the film we saw last week?' His mum smiled.

'Yes. So he must be a spy.'

'He's a spy,' Vera said loyally.

'What makes you think Mr Kolenski's got a wireless like that?' their mum asked.

'I saw the case.'

'Oh, yes,' she said, raising her eyebrows to show that she knew he was playing one of his games.

'It's true. I saw it in his room.'

'What were you doing up there?'

'I waited until he went out to the dustbin then ...'

Alf watched a frown begin to form on his mum's forehead. He ploughed on desperately. 'He doesn't know I've been in his flat. Vera kept watch for me. I only saw the suitcase as he was coming back…'

'What have I told you about going into the guests' rooms?'

'But this was different…'

'I specially told you to leave Mr Kolenski in peace, didn't I?'

'But he's a spy.'

'He's a Polish refugee.' His mum said the words very clearly, as if Alf was an idiot. 'A refugee. Do you know what that is?'

Alf nodded. 'But…'

'He only just managed to escape the Nazis.' His mum glared at him. 'He's been very ill and the last thing he wants is a stupid boy who's seen too many war films making his life a misery.'

'But what about the wireless?' Alf protested.

'What did you really see? No exaggerating.'

'Well, there was this suitcase with a wireless in it.'

'You really saw a wireless?'

'Well, the case wasn't open, but there

was a wire sticking out of it.'

'I thought as much. It's all your imagination.' His mum sighed hopelessly. 'What would he be spying on in this house? He's too ill to work and he never goes further than the corner shop. Use a bit of common sense.'

Alf and Vera retreated to their den at the end of the garden.

'I was sure he was a spy,' Alf said.

'Me too,' Vera agreed.

'But perhaps Mum's right.' Alf looked fed up. 'The Poles hate the Germans since they invaded their country, so why would Mr Kolenski help them?'

Vera put on a fed-up expression like her big brother.

'Anyway, what would he spy on?'

Suddenly Alf's mouth fell open, then it closed in a determined line. 'Of course!' he exclaimed. 'What can we see from our front window?'

'The beach,' Vera said.

'Yes, and ships leaving port and going out to sea – the same as he can see from his window! He could tell the Germans when any ships passed and the U-boats could wait to sink them.'

Alf glanced at Vera. She was frowning hard.

'U-boats are German submarines,' he explained. 'You know that, don't you?'

She nodded vigorously. 'Oh, yes. I know that, Alf.'

It was obvious now that he'd thought of it. The spy was telling the Germans when the ships came in and out of the port and what they were carrying. The German U-boat wolf packs could then try to sink the ships as they passed.

'Without those ships bringing supplies of food, we'd starve,' Alf told Vera. He ran his fingers through his spiky ginger hair. 'And you know who sails on one of those ships, don't you?'

She knew that all right. 'Our dad,' Vera said solemnly.

3 Alf is betrayed

'Mr Kolenski must be stopped,' Alf told Vera. 'It's up to us.'

'What're we going to do, Alf?'

'We're going to tell the Home Guard,' Alf declared.

Vera's eyes opened wide in admiration. 'Can I come with you?'

'All right,' Alf agreed. 'But leave the talking to me.'

They left their den and set off down the road towards the town. Their house had been a guest-house for holiday-makers before the war, but now no one wanted to come to the seaside, so the only people renting rooms were Mr Kolenski, who had escaped from Poland, and Mr and Mrs Green, whose own house had been bombed.

Alf and Vera walked along the empty promenade and looked longingly at the beach. They couldn't play there any more because it was covered in endless loops of barbed wire and concrete blocks and twisted iron girders, all intended to stop German troops landing.

Secretly, he hoped that if the Germans did invade they would choose his beach, because then he'd have a grandstand view of the battle from his front window. He felt a bit ashamed of this wish because he thought it might be unpatriotic.

'Where are we going?' Vera asked, interrupting his thoughts.

'To see Mr Harding,' Alf said. 'He's the Home Guard Captain.'

'Oh,' Vera said. 'Are we nearly there?'

'You know that shop on the corner with the painted windows so that you can't see in?'

Vera nodded.

'Well, that's Mr Harding's office. He's a solicitor.'

'Will they let us in?'

Alf had been worrying about this himself but he said confidently, 'When I tell them it's Home Guard business, they will.'

'Is Captain Harding in the army?'

'Not exactly.' Alf wasn't quite sure of the difference between the army and the Home Guard. 'The Home Guard is a sort of part-time army for people who are too old for the proper army – I think.'

'Oh,' Vera said. 'Well, where's our proper army?'

Alf found that he wasn't sure of this either. 'They're at secret camps. You're not supposed to know in case you accidentally say and a spy overhears you.'

'Like Mr Kolenski.'

'Yes. Then he'd use his transmitter to tell the Germans and they'd bomb the camp.' Alf felt that he'd explained that quite well.

They reached the shop, and its blank windows with their crosses of brown tape to stop bomb blast looked more forbidding than usual. Alf pushed the door open and led Vera inside. There was a lady with her hair in a bun sitting at a table. She was wearing a coat so that she didn't need the fire on, as everyone was supposed to save fuel.

'We've come to see Captain Harding about Home Guard business,' Alf announced. He was surprised by how confident he sounded.

A few minutes later they were standing
in front of Mr Harding's desk. He was a
big man in a dark suit, but he seemed quite
friendly.

'Well, what can I do for you two?' he
asked.

Alf told him everything about Mr
Kolenski. Captain Harding made some
notes on a piece of paper and said, 'Leave
everything to me. I'll make sure the proper
authorities are informed. You did the right
thing, coming to me.'

Alf and Vera left his office feeling proud of themselves.

They went home and waited, but the days crawled by and nothing happened. No army trucks came screaming up the street filled with soldiers. No doors were smashed in with rifle butts. Nothing happened which was in the least like the films Alf had seen. Instead, Mr Kolenski limped to the corner shop each morning and life carried on as usual.

Alf wondered whether Captain Harding had only been pretending to take them seriously. Grown-ups were always doing that.

Then a week later, their mum entered the living room with one of her furious frowns chiselled into her forehead.

'What did I tell you about Mr Kolenski?' she demanded.

'He's a refugee,' Alf suggested.

'I told you to leave him alone, didn't I?'

Alf and Vera nodded. 'We've not been upstairs,' Alf said.

'No, you've been to the Home Guard,' their mum exploded. 'You've been telling everyone he's a spy. He's got enough to worry about without silly kids trying to make trouble for him.'

She paused for a second, then went on in a different voice. 'He left Poland because his family was arrested by the Nazis. He doesn't know what's happened to them. He was the only one to escape.'

'Oh,' Alf said, because he couldn't think of anything else. 'How did you know...?'

'That you'd been to the Home Guard?' his mum finished for him. 'Because a policeman came round here to tell me not to worry. They knew all about Mr Kolenski. They always check up on refugees very carefully.'

The next time Alf stepped out of the

door, he almost bumped into Mr Kolenski on the stairs. Alf smiled weakly.

'You a *gut* boy, Alf,' Mr Kolenski said. 'You love your country.'

Alf noticed how Mr Kolenski always said 'gut' instead of 'good', just like the Germans in the war films. He was still convinced that Mr Kolenski was a spy.

'We've got to catch him red-handed,' Alf told Vera. 'If we could surprise him sending a message or something, they'd have to believe us.'

Vera gazed at her brother confidently. 'What shall we do next, Alf?'

4 The hunt begins!

Alf switched off his bedroom light. The room was very dark because of the blackout curtains. He'd been told that the pilot of a bomber could see a single chink of light from miles away and use it as a target to unload his bombs.

Alf felt his way round the furniture until he reached the window. He lifted up the curtain and stood behind it. On moonlit nights he could sometimes see the outlines of ships steaming towards the port. Once he'd even recognised his dad's ship. Tonight the moon was hidden by racing clouds.

Overhead he heard Mr Kolenski's footsteps. He often limped backwards and forwards for hours. Mum said that he was probably thinking about the family he'd left behind in Poland.

Suddenly the footsteps changed their rhythm. They strode across the room then ceased. He'd gone on to the landing. Perhaps he was going to make a cup of tea, Alf thought. But a second later he heard a stair creak, then another. Mr Kolenski was going out!

Alf's heart began to beat faster. Mr Kolenski never went out at night.

Alf pressed his face against the window. The door below clicked very softly and at that moment the clouds parted. By the light of the moon he saw Mr Kolenski trot quickly down the front steps. Alf gasped. Mr Kolenski wasn't limping!

Alf held his breath. As the dark shape passed the white gatepost he saw the outline of what looked like a small suitcase. Then Alf saw Mr Kolenski's shadow on the road, walking swiftly away from town.

Alf acted quickly. He ran into Vera's room and shook her awake.

Vera moaned.

'Don't make a sound. Mr Kolenski's gone out. I'm going to follow him.'

Vera was instantly awake. She jumped out of bed. 'Can I come?'

'No. Listen. I want you to keep watch through my window. If Mr Kolenski comes back, and I don't, you tell Mum to get the Home Guard to come and search for me.'

Alf ran downstairs while Vera tiptoed into his bedroom and took up her position behind the curtain.

The moon had disappeared again. Alf ran in the direction Mr Kolenski had taken.

Every so often he paused to listen. At last he heard footsteps hurrying along ahead of him. He was sure they were Mr Kolenski's. He slowed down so as not to get too near.

They went past the last of the houses and came to the sand dunes. Alf was finding it harder to see around him. He could hear waves breaking on the shore. The barbed wire was invisible, but he knew it was there. He and Vera had often searched for a beach where there wasn't any, but it seemed to them that every beach in England was covered in it.

The next time Alf paused to listen for the footsteps, they had disappeared. There was only one way Mr Kolenski could have gone and that was into the sand dunes. Alf strained his eyes and ears but could detect nothing. He was just wondering how he could find anyone among all those tiny sand hills when he saw a glimmer of light.

Alf slid into the soft sand and began to snake forward. It was almost like swimming except for the occasional stones which bruised his fingers. He reached the top of a dune and looked down into a dip. Mr Kolenski was crouched over the open suitcase.

Alf could see the spy's face in the light

reflected from a small torch which he was holding in his mouth. He was shining it into the case. There was no wireless in it. Instead there was a small shovel which was in two parts. Mr Kolenski took it out. The blade was tied to the handle with a piece of wire so that it wouldn't get lost. Mr Kolenski slotted the parts together to make a short spade.

Alf was amazed. He'd been so certain there was a wireless in the case that he wondered for a moment if there could be two cases. Then he wondered what Mr Kolenski was going to do. Did he sneak out at night to build secret sand castles?

Mr Kolenski looked at his watch and took the torch out of his mouth. He stood up, pointed the torch out to sea and switched it on and off three times.

Alf gasped out loud but Mr Kolenski was too busy to notice. Suddenly, there was one tiny blip of light from out at sea. Alf's head whirled with thoughts. He'd been right all the time. Mr Kolenski was a spy.

5 Spycatcher!

Mr Kolenski dropped the torch into the case, took off his coat and climbed over the sand dunes towards the sea. A second later there were swishing sounds. Alf couldn't think what was happening, then there was a clink as the metal of the spade hit a stone and everything became clear. Mr Kolenski was digging. A boat was coming to fetch him. He was digging a trench under the barbed wire. The spy was going to escape.

Alf thought quickly. He had to get help. If he ran to the Home Guard headquarters in town, it would take him so long that by the time he got there Mr Kolenski would have crawled under the barbed wire and escaped. There must be a quicker way than that. An idea came to him. If he could get the torch, he could point it towards the town and wave it about. There was always someone on the lookout for people breaking the blackout. A light would get someone's attention.

He squirmed up the sand dune, slid down the other side and cautiously put his hand into the suitcase. As his fingers touched the torch the moon came out from behind the clouds again.

He looked over the edge of the dune and saw the shape of Mr Kolenski digging hurriedly. He heard him panting. Alf glanced up and his mouth fell open. Against the horizon was engraved the black outline of a U-boat; that was how he was going to escape.

Then he heard something much nearer scrape on the beach. At first he couldn't see what it was, then his eyes found the outline of a dinghy with three figures in it. One of them stepped ashore. Alf realised that he'd got everything wrong again.

Mr Kolenski wasn't escaping, he was helping someone else get into the country: another spy or a saboteur to plant bombs.

Now what should he do? He had to stop Mr Kolenski getting to the other side of the barbed wire.

Alf's fingers closed round the torch.

Bluff, he thought. He'd seen a film where a boy had captured a spy using a piece of wood. He'd jabbed it in the spy's back and pretended it was a pistol. Then he'd marched him to the police station. Well, he would bluff Mr Kolenski into thinking he was armed.

Alf stood up.

'Hands up!' he shouted, and switched on the torch. The startled face of Mr Kolenski stared from the middle of a coil of barbed wire. Alf tried to make his voice deeper. 'This is the Home Guard,' he shouted, hoping that he couldn't be seen behind the torch. 'Drop your spade and put up your hands. We've got you covered.'

But Mr Kolenski did not do as Alf told him; instead he dropped his spade and pulled something out of his trouser pocket. Alf recognised it immediately – a German Luger pistol. He'd seen them often enough in his comics.

'No, no…!' cried Mr Kolenski.

Alf didn't wait for him to finish. He dived into the sand dune. As he landed, his hand felt a cricket ball-sized stone. Without thinking, he grabbed it and threw it at the spot where Mr Kolenski was standing.

There was a crack as the pistol went off and a second later rifle fire came up the beach from the direction of the dinghy.

The noise was deafening. Alf pressed himself into the bottom of the sand dune. Through the rifle fire he heard Mr Kolenski shouting, 'Nicht schiessen!' He guessed that the words probably meant, 'Don't shoot!'

The firing ceased. As Alf's ears returned to normal he heard a hissing sound. He was puzzled for a moment, then he realised what had happened. His stone must have hit Mr Kolenski, and when he fired, the bullet had gone wild and punctured the dinghy. It was going down! Now they wouldn't be able to escape back to the U-boat.

But what was he going to do next? It was up to him to stop the enemy, but his mind was blank.

At that instant he heard the sound of a lorry racing along the road. Could he stop it and get help, he wondered? But if he stood up, Mr Kolenski would see his outline and he'd be shot. He was trapped in the dune.

Suddenly the lorry skidded to a halt. The next second a spotlight lit up the beach and a voice shouted. 'This is the Home Guard. Drop your weapons!'

Alf recognised Captain Harding's voice.

He poked his head over the edge of the dune again. A lorry was parked at an odd angle and the spotlight mounted on it lit up the three men on the beach. They all had their hands up.

Suddenly orders were shouted and men ran past Alf as if he didn't exist. Two members of the Home Guard dragged Mr Kolenski out of his trench and others made a gap in the barbed wire. Two German sailors

marched through with their hands on their heads.

The third man was in ordinary clothes and carried a suitcase. He looked as though he had just got off a train. Alf studied him carefully, but there was nothing unusual about him. No one would ever notice him in a crowd. He was undoubtedly a spy. Alf wondered whether it would be unpatriotic to ask him for his autograph, but before he had decided, the spy had been put in the back of the lorry and driven off.

Captain Harding came up to Alf and slapped him on the shoulder. 'All right, young man?' he asked.

Alf nodded.

'I expect it's a long time since you've been all the way down to the sea,' Captain Harding said. 'Would you like to see what our friends have left on the beach for us?'

'Can I?' Alf asked excitedly.

They went through the gap in the barbed wire and Alf helped Captain Harding pull the punctured German dinghy up the beach. There were only some paddles in it, but Alf was not disappointed. He was thinking about what he would tell his friends the next morning.

'I think we'd better take you back to your mum,' Captain Harding said. 'She's waiting at Home Guard headquarters.'

6 Alf's souvenir

When Alf finally arrived at Home Guard headquarters it was three o'clock in the morning. The headquarters was in the amusement arcade on the sea front, which was boarded up for the war. He found his mum and Vera waiting for him.

'Mr Kolenski was a spy,' he started to say. 'He had a Luger…'

His mum grabbed hold of him and shook him. She had tears in her eyes. 'What do you mean by going out at night?' she demanded, in a choking voice. Then she hugged him to her.

'I told you he was a spy,' Alf mumbled, his face pressed into his mum's coat.

'D'you know how worried I've been?' she asked, sniffing.

Alf thought that if he sniffed like that he'd be told to use his handkerchief. He looked up and saw that his mum was crying.

'I'm all right,' he said.

'Oh, I know you are,' his mum said, and gave him another hug. 'I'm proud of you really, and I'm sorry I didn't believe you. But you still shouldn't go out at night. I can't bear to think what might have happened.' Her voice rose. 'You could have been shot. I'd never have forgiven myself.'

She gave him a half shake, half hug.

Alf found himself shivering for some reason and hugged her back.

Captain Harding smiled. 'I think we could all do with a nice hot mug of cocoa,' he said. 'It was a good job you alerted us to what was going on,' he told Alf's mum. 'That meant we were on the scene pretty quickly – before Alf was in any real danger.'

'But I thought I heard shooting…' Alf's mum started to say.

'One or two people getting over-excited. That was all.'

Captain Harding took her arm to lead her to his office at the back of the arcade. He looked over his shoulder and winked at Alf.

Vera and Alf stopped to pull faces at themselves in the crazy mirrors which lined the corridor. They changed from fat to thin to tall to short.

Vera whispered to Alf, 'I'm sorry, I told Mum where you'd gone. She found me out of bed and made me tell.'

'That's all right. I'm glad you did, because otherwise the Home Guard wouldn't have arrived so quickly.'

'What happened?'

'I'll tell you all about it when we get home,' Alf promised. Suddenly he felt tired. 'Let's have our cocoa now.'

Ten minutes later, Captain Harding said goodnight, and Alf and Vera and their mum were taken home, wrapped in army blankets in the Home Guard lorry.

'Well, you caught your spy,' their mum said when they were back in their house.

'What will happen to him?' Alf asked.

'I expect he will be put in prison.'

'Won't they shoot him?'

'I don't think so.' She sighed. 'You know, I feel quite sorry for poor Mr Kolenski.'

'But he was a German spy,' Alf protested.

'Yes, he was,' their mum agreed tiredly.

'But do you know why?'

'Because he's a German.'

'No, he's not.' She shook her head. 'He's Polish, just as he always said.'

'Well, why was he helping the Germans?'

'He told Captain Harding that it was because of his family. The Nazis arrested his wife and children and threatened to shoot them unless he worked for them.'

'He still shouldn't have helped them,' Alf said.

His mum ruffled his hair. 'Bedtime,' she said sadly.

When he was in bed she said, 'Goodnight, my hero,' and gave him a hug. 'Sometimes it's not easy to know what is the right thing to do, you know.' She switched out the light. 'What would you have done if you'd been Mr Kolenski?' she asked from the door.

Alf lay in bed. It seemed very quiet without Mr Kolenski's footsteps limping up and down above his head. All that was left to remind him of Mr Kolenski was his small suitcase. The Home Guard had let him keep it and now it stood at the foot of the bed. He didn't know why, but he felt glad that he had it.

He thought about what his mum had said and tried to imagine what it would be like if she and Vera were arrested. If he refused to help the Nazis, they'd shoot his family; if he agreed to help them, he'd be like Mr Kolenski. For a while he wondered what he would do. Then he hoped he would never have to find out.

Alf the spycatcher fell asleep.

Do you think Mr Kolenski was right to spy for the Germans?

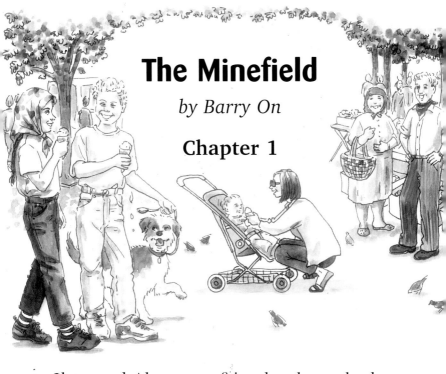

The Minefield

by Barry On

Chapter 1

Ilma and Alen were friends; always had
been, almost from the time they were born
just a few weeks apart on neighbouring
farms. As soon as they were old enough to
run, they would run together through the
summer meadows filled with wild flowers.
Now they were older, they went fishing
together on the banks of the river that ran
along the bottom of the valley or climbed
the trees in the woodland that crested the
hill above the field of growing crops. And
always, in the distance, were the high
mountains that they loved so much. The
villagers smiled at them and called them

'the inseparables' – almost like brother and sister – almost like twins.

Ilma was just as strong and agile as her companion. She could throw as far, run as far, run as fast. Perhaps Alen was a little better at climbing trees, but Ilma was the better swimmer. But there was no competition between them – no rivalry. They would laugh at the same things and their laughter was easy, frequent and never unkind. A lot of the time they had no need to talk; each knew without any words exactly what the other was thinking and agreed with it. They were true friends.

They did have one other constant playfellow. He could certainly run faster then either of them and was a good swimmer. But he couldn't throw and he couldn't climb trees. His name was Rikki. He was Alen's dog.

At first Ilma and Alen took little notice of the talk of war. They knew that both lots of parents were worried and that they would discuss the situation in low and troubled voices in their different houses once the children were in bed. But to the children, war was only talk. It would surely never come to their lovely, peaceful valley.

But one day there were soldiers in drab, camouflaged uniforms and steel helmets moving along the road alongside the river. Then came the tanks, churning up the surface of the road as they lumbered like dangerous, armour-clad insects in search of their unseen prey. Sometimes the sound of shelling could be heard in the distance and sometimes, nearer, the crackle of rifle fire.

Ilma's parents became more withdrawn and went less often into the village. The few visitors who came to the farm now were different from their former friends and there was much less laughter.

Chapter 2

One cold winter's day the soldiers came and laid mines in the big field that bordered the two farms. Ilma and Alen watched in silence as the truck carrying the mines moved slowly backward and forwards across the snow-patched field with the mine layers walking behind planting the little mines into the fertile soil. It was a field that had once grown fine crops of root vegetables. So often the two children

had watched their neighbour at work
sowing turnips or beet. But what was being
sown now would never yield a healthy
crop. And it would be a long time before
anyone worked that soil again.

It was a few days after the laying of the minefield that the unthinkable happened – the impossible.

Alen was late at their meeting place, near the river. When he came at last, his face was set in an angry scowl.

'What's the matter?' asked Ilma in concern.

He glared at her as though she had in some way insulted him. 'I can't see you any more,' he muttered grimly. 'We can't be friends any more.'

Ilma did not understand. The words made no sense. 'How can we not be friends?' she asked in wonder. 'There is nothing that could stop me from being your friend, Alen.'

'It's the war,' he said flatly.

She was still puzzled. 'We're not at war, Alen. Not you and me. How could we be?'

'Our people are at war, you know that. You are on the other side, Ilma. Don't you understand?'

'No, I don't. I do know there are people in the village who have been friends for life who no longer talk to each other because they belong to different religions, different races. But that's stupid, isn't it?

They are still the same people that they always have been. And so are we.'

Rikki the dog was miserably aware that something was wrong between the two people he worshipped most in all the world. He put his paw up to Ilma and tried to lick her hand. She fondled his ear, absent-mindedly.

'Down, Rikki,' commanded Alen harshly. The dog lay down obediently, his head between his paws, but he continued to watch them with melancholy eyes.

'You are a girl, Ilma,' continued Alen. 'You don't understand.'

Ilma froze. It was the worst thing he could have said. Never before had he implied that girls were inferior to boys in any way. It had just never arisen; not with her and Alen. She thought she would have been less hurt if he had slapped her in the face. At least then she could have hit him back. Now she was too sad even to be angry.

'So now we are at war?' asked Ilma.

'Yes.'

'And I am the enemy?'

He shrugged his shoulders.

'Are you going to kill me?' she asked.

'Of course not. We don't kill girls.'

'Really? Are you so sure? What about my father, then? Would you kill him?'

Again he shrugged. 'War is hard, Ilma. People get hurt. Some get killed. That is how war is.'

'And are you going to fight? To kill?'

'As soon as I am old enough. I have to, don't you see? I have to fight for my people.'

Ilma stared across at the snow-capped mountains far beyond the river valley. There were vapour trails high above them. She heard the noise of muffled shelling like the mutter of distant summer thunder from a clear sky.

'No, I don't see. I don't understand. War means hate, I *do* know that. And I could never hate you, Alen. Whatever happens.'

He sighed. 'It's different for girls. I knew you wouldn't understand.'

He turned and walked away. Rikki slunk at his heels glancing backwards towards Ilma to see if, as always before, she would come with them. Ilma did not move. There were hot tears in her eyes, but she blinked them back. The long day stretched emptily ahead of her. Now she was alone.

Ilma asked her father to explain what had happened. He was gruff. 'Alen is right.

It is better that you don't see him again.'

She turned to her mother for help but no help came. 'It's an ancient quarrel, Ilma. It has to do with governments and history and old enmities. It is the way things are. There is nothing people like us can do about it.'

Alen was right. She did not understand.

Chapter 3

Ilma rarely went into the village after that. On the few occasions that she encountered Alen, he walked by as though he had not seen her, as though she did not exist. Only Rikki would look pleadingly at her, longing for her to join them in a race through the meadow or a swim in the cool waters of the river.

Ilma walked alone that summer. She wandered through the woods along the crest of the hill or followed the winding paths along the river. She kept away from the main roads with their spasmodic processions of troops or armoured vehicles. And, of course, she avoided the big field with its barren crop of deadly, hidden mines.

One morning, she saw Alen sporting with Rikki in the meadow below the field. He was throwing a stick for the dog to chase and fetch back to him. She could tell that Alen was laughing in a way that she herself had not laughed for many days.

The dog was bounding through the wild flowers and the scarlet poppies as though there were no cares in the world.

Suddenly a rabbit broke cover in the meadow immediately in front of Rikki. At once the dog swerved and gave chase. A live prey was better than a dead stick any day. The rabbit raced through a gap in the hedge and made off across the big field, its white scut bobbing in the sunlight. Rikki followed. Far away, Ilma gave a stifled cry of fear and warning.

'Rikki!' yelled Alen urgently. 'Stay! Down!'

But Rikki had almost caught the rabbit and, though normally obedient to the boy's commands, no words could halt him now.

It was not a loud explosion. Just a dull thud like the sound of a sledgehammer on a door. It was not a bright flash. Just a sudden flicker of light, momentarily brighter than the sunlight. When it was over the rabbit lay dead. And Rikki, the dog, was lying still.

'Rikki!' shouted Alen. 'Rikki! Get up! Come back!'

There was no response from the dog.

Alen ran to the edge of the field. Ilma

also began to run. 'No, Alen!' she called desperately. 'Wait!' But he could not hear her.

He scrambled through the gap in the hedge and shouted again to his dog. Rikki raised his head from the ground and gave a desolate whimper, a cry for help. Alen immediately set off towards him. Ilma ran as hard as she could but the way to the field was uphill. There was cold fear in her throat and her breath came in sobs. For the moment the hedge hid Alen from her view.

Then she heard the second thud of an exploding mine. Now the fear clutched her heart and she groaned with despair. 'Alen!'

She reached the edge of the minefield and stared desperately across. Alen had almost reached his dog before the second mine exploded. He was sitting on the ground holding his leg. His face was ashen white. Dark blood seeped through his trouser leg.

'Are you all right?' A silly question to ask, but she was torn between distress at his injury and an overwhelming relief that he was still alive. He looked up towards her. 'Stay away!' he said, dully. 'Keep out. It's dangerous.'

'I can see that,' she answered. 'Can you walk?'

He tried to rise, but fell back again to the ground. 'It's my leg,' he said helplessly. 'I think it's broken. And there's all this blood.' His voice was hoarse with fear and shock. 'Get help, Ilma. Quickly. I need help. Fetch my father.'

Ilma was decisive. 'No time to get help. You're bleeding too much. I'm coming in.'

Chapter 4

Ilma squeezed through the gap in the hedge and stood on the very edge of the perilous field. She thought for a moment and then turned and went back into the meadow. Alen gave an involuntary sob of despair as she disappeared from his sight. Ilma walked through the wild flowers and gathered an armful of scarlet poppies. If she managed to succeed in finding a path to Alen, she might at least mark the way back. No sense in making the journey doubly dangerous. Then she picked up the stick that Alen had been throwing to Rikki such a short time ago and stuck it in the waistband of her trousers. She returned to the field, slipped cautiously back through the gap in the hedge, and looked about her.

Everything was still and silent. There was no sound of distant gunfire, no rumble of war vehicles along the far-off road. It was as though time was standing still, watching her, waiting to see what she would do. Ilma took a deep breath and set off towards the fallen figure of Alen.

She trod very lightly on the ground. That was not likely to make any difference if she did step on a mine, but it seemed more sensible not to be too heavy-footed.

If she were very careful, and more than a little lucky, she reckoned she could probably tell where the mines had been laid. The mine layers, in their haste to complete an unpopular and hazardous task as quickly as they could, had not been very thorough in their attempts to conceal the mines. In some places they had not been completely covered and it was still possible to make out a dull, khaki-coloured rim beneath an inadequate scattering of soil. In other places, circles of yellowing grass, or unnatural hummocks were tell-tale signs. If she kept to the longer grass, moved slowly and examined very inch of ground before she moved, she would probably be all right – probably.

So Ilma stepped carefully through the sunlight of the field. All her senses were at full stretch. The colours of the world about her seemed unnaturally bright and she could smell the heavy scent of the poppies that she carried. She no longer walked in silence. All around her she could hear the busy hum of insects: the drone of bees and the higher-pitched buzz of flies. Blue and orange butterflies danced around her, alighting from time to time on the patches of weed that now grew in the once cultivated field. One even landed on the visible surface of a half-concealed mine and spread wide its delicate wings, attracted no doubt by the greater warmth of the plastic. Ilma watched it with envy.

'Lucky thing,' she thought. 'You don't have to watch where you go. You are not going to explode a mine just by stepping on it.'

Every few yards she laid down a scarlet poppy to show where she had, so far,

walked with safety. The sun was hot on her back and she could feel a trickle of sweat down her spine. But her brain was ice-cold. She felt frightened, certainly, but at the same time curiously detached. She had no thoughts about being brave. From the moment she had seen Alen lying wounded in the field, she knew she had no alternative.

At last she reached Alen. He was still deathly white and his left trouser leg was oozing with blood. But his first thought was for his dog.

'Rikki,' he pleaded. 'Help Rikki.'

Ilma looked across at the still body. She shook her head. 'Rikki is dead,' she said in a flat voice. 'We can't help him now.'

Alen gave a short sob that seemed to have more anger in it than sorrow. 'We can't leave him here.'

'We must,' Ilma told him. 'I'll try to get you out. But I can't come back. Not for Rikki. He's dead.' She looked down at him. 'Can you stand?'

He tried. A wince of pain came into his eyes, but he bit his lip hard to prevent any cry escaping. 'No. It's no good. You'd better get help.'

Ilma took off her cotton scarf and knotted it as tightly as she could around the thigh of the broken leg. Then she pushed the stick between the leg and the scarf and twisted it to tighten the binding still further. 'That should help to stop the bleeding.' She stood and considered the situation. 'You were pretty lucky, really.'

'Oh yes,' said Alen with gritted teeth. 'Very lucky.'

'You trod on a mine. You could have been killed. As it is, you probably won't even lose your leg. You'll just have a limp for life. And a scar – a war wound. You'll be proud of that.'

She knelt and put her arms under his legs. 'If you can't walk, I'll have to carry you. You're not that heavy.'

The pain of being lifted must have been agony to Alen, but he made no sound.

'Put your arms round my neck.'

He obeyed, but there was no warmth in the action.

Very slowly Ilma carried the wounded boy back along the trail of fallen poppies. Despite her words, the load was a heavy one and she could no longer tread lightly. She reached the gap in the hedge, staggered through and set Alen down on the grass. Then she sat down beside him and felt suddenly very tired.

There was a shout from the farmhouses away at the bottom of the meadow. Alen's father had seen them emerge from the minefield, and although he had no way of knowing exactly what had happened, he knew that something was wrong. Now he was hurrying up the field towards them.

'You'll be all right now,' said Ilma wearily.

Alen made no reply.

'I'm sorry about Rikki,' Ilma continued. 'Really sorry.' She had loved the dog just as much as Alen had.

Alen looked at her. His eyes were dull with pain and his mouth was twisted with bitterness. 'This makes no difference, you know,' he muttered harshly. 'You are still the other side. Nothing has changed.'

Alen's father arrived. He looked at his son and then glanced briefly at Ilma. In the old days he had always been jolly and talkative. Now he said nothing. He took Alen in his powerful arms and set off at a trot towards his home. Neither he nor his son looked back.

Ilma rose to her feet. She looked out over the river towards the beautiful mountains. They looked as they always looked, but she knew that Alen's last words to her were wrong – utterly wrong.

Everything had changed.

At the end of the story Ilma said, 'everything had changed'. In what ways had everything changed?